W9-BRW-547

Jennifer Armstrong

KING CROW

illustrated by Eric Rohmann

CROWN PUBLISHERS, INC., NEW YORK

Nell Cummins School Library
Corte Madera, Calif.

Text copyright © 1995 by Jennifer Armstrong
Illustrations copyright © 1995 by Eric Rohmann

All rights reserved. No part of this book may be
reproduced or transmitted in any form or by any
means, electronic or mechanical, including
photocopying, recording, or by any information
storage and retrieval system, without permission
in writing from the publisher.

Published by Crown Publishers, Inc., a Random
House company, 201 East 50th Street, New York,
New York 10022

CROWN is a trademark of Crown Publishers, Inc.

Manufactured in Singapore

Library of Congress Cataloging-in-Publication Data
Armstrong, Jennifer, 1961–
King Crow / by Jennifer Armstrong ; illustrated by
Eric Rohmann.
p.   cm.
Summary: Jailed by an evil foe, a king receives
invaluable help from a crow that regularly brings
him the latest news.
[1. Crows—Fiction. 2. Kings, queens, rulers, etc.—
Fiction.]
I. Rohmann, Eric, ill. II. Title.
PZ7.A77367Ki   1995
[E]—dc20
93-39261

ISBN 0-517-59634-2 (trade)
      0-517-59635-0 (lib. bdg.)

10 9 8 7 6 5 4 3 2 1   First Edition

ONCE
THERE WAS
a wise and generous king,
slow to anger and very fair.
His name was Cormac,
and his people loved him.

But the neighboring king, Bregant, did not love him, and by constant harrying
and pillaging of Cormac's lands and people, goaded Cormac into war.

Reluctantly, Cormac readied his armies. But by bribe and threat, some of Cormac's generals were persuaded to turn the battle against their own king. By such evil tricks, the balance was tipped in Bregant's favor, and devastation followed. Cormac was unhorsed and, cracking his head, lost himself in darkness. He was left for dead on the field, and the tyrant carried the day, scattering Cormac's ragged army.

When Cormac awoke on the morning after the battle, he knew he was alone, but he could not see. The blow to his head had blinded him. He cried, sure that his people were slaughtered and his city taken. Near despair, he wandered into the woods and sat under a tree to mourn.

Then he heard a crow, croaking weakly nearby. Cormac put out his hands and felt torn and ragged feathers. Through one wing was an arrow, shot from the thick of battle.

"We had no quarrel with you," Cormac said.

"Be merciful, King," the crow begged.

"I will," the king replied, and gently pulled the arrow from the crow's wing.

With two clumsy jumps, the crow hopped away, stretching its wounded wing. "Much better," it croaked. "I'll thank you for this, and you'll be glad of it."

Cormac smiled, but he took no comfort from the crow's promise. Closing his sightless eyes, he fell asleep.

He awoke to the sound of stamping hooves, shouts, and harness iron. In a moment, he was surrounded by Bregant's soldiers, taken prisoner, and led away to be locked in the tower of his own castle.

"This is your entire kingdom now," said Bregant, slamming the door and throwing the bolt.

Cormac paced the stone-walled room with his hands outstretched, and tipped his face to the barred windows. He heard a stumbling flutter of wings and then felt the grip of claws on his shoulder.

"I'll help you, King," the crow said. "I'll be your eyes. I'll get you out. I'll kill your enemy and restore your kingdom."

"Thank you, Crow," Cormac said. "I do thank you, but I don't believe you can."

"Can't I?" the crow said with a creaking laugh. It flapped its ragged wings and left the tower, and Cormac was left alone to brood.

Night fell. Cormac sat, remembering his friends and his family, and hoping without hope that they were not all murdered or imprisoned. His world was now just one silent stone room. When, before dawn, he heard the rustle of wings high above his head, he held out his hands in gratitude.

"My friend, Crow," he said. "What news?"

The crow perched on Cormac's shoulder and cleared its raspy throat. "I've been out among the people, sitting on window sills, flying by the stables, perching outside doorways. And this is what I've seen.

"The tyrant feasts in your own hall, a knife thrust scornfully into the back of your chair. And there he sits, drinking from your cup, laughing."

With a flutter of ragged feathers, the crow was gone.

When Cormac's jailers came with food, the blind king raised his voice.

"Tell me," he said. "Is it true that Bregant drinks from my cup and sits in my chair?"

The jailers laughed. "Easy guesswork. Any conqueror does as much."

"Is a knife plunged into that chair?" Cormac continued.

A startled silence met this speech. Then, one jailer came close. "How did you know that? You're blind, and no one has come here to speak to you."

"Perhaps it was a dream that I had," Cormac answered softly. "Perhaps I can see better now than I did before. And perhaps that knife will have its work to do."

Cormac leaned against the wall and turned his face up to the windows. He heard the jailers leave and wondered what would happen next.

At the following dawn, Cormac heard the flap of wings above him and held out his hand for the crow to perch on. "What news, Crow?" Cormac asked.

The crow cleared its raspy throat. "I've been out among the people, sitting on window sills, flying by the stables, perching outside doorways. And this is what I've seen.

"Bregant was visited by a poet last night, who sang of great battles, and of a king who died when his horse stumbled on a molehill and threw him."

And with another shuffle and racket of its tattered wings, the crow flew off.

Neil Cummins School Library
Corte Madera, Calif.

When Cormac's jailers came in with food, their steps were not so bold as the day before.

"Tell me," said Cormac. "Did Bregant entertain a poet in my hall last night?"

"Another easy guess," one of the men replied. "It happens often."

"Did that poet sing of battles, and of a king killed by a mole?" Cormac continued.

"Another dream?" asked one of the men uneasily.

"Tell Bregant that perhaps that mole will have its work to do," Cormac said, and turned his blind face away.

The jailers left in a hurry, their feet clattering down the stone steps of the tower. Cormac paced his cell through the dark day and the dark night, thinking and waiting for the crow to return.

With the dawn, he heard the flap of wings. He jumped up from his seat. "What news, Crow?"

The crow cleared its raspy throat. "I've been out among the people, sitting on window sills, flying by the stables, perching outside doorways. And this is what I've seen.

"The tyrant went hunting yesterday, taking your longbow with him. And as he aimed for a boar in the woods, the bow, which was strung too tight, broke in two."

"Thank you, Crow," Cormac said.

"Thanks to you, King," the crow replied. "My debt is honored, and I'll be going."

The crow stretched its wings and flapped to the windows. But there it paused.

"I see one more thing from where I sit," the crow said. "The hill on the horizon is crowned with fire."

"Who makes this fire?" Cormac asked.

"I do not know." Then the crow jumped from the sill and was gone.

When Cormac's jailers came, the blind king heard the footsteps of another man with them. He guessed who it was.

"Tell me," he said to his jailers. "Did Bregant go hunting yesterday with my longbow? And did the bow break in two as the tyrant aimed for the boar?"

An angry shout filled the room. "How do you know these things?" Bregant demanded, taking Cormac by the throat. "On three days you've told my soldiers what you could not see. Tell me what you know!"

"I'll tell you that perhaps my bow will have its work to do," Cormac said, feeling the hot breath of the other man on his face.

The tyrant threw Cormac away from him. His voice shook. "So far you've seen only what has happened already. But you can't see what will happen in the future. Tell me that, and you will go free."

Cormac had no faith that his enemy would honor such a promise, even if he could see the future. But he knew the crow was gone, so he must make use of the help he'd been given. He thought hard as the men locked the cell door and then called out to stop them.

"Wait," Cormac said, holding up one hand. "I can tell you what will happen after this."

Bregant and the guards returned, eyeing one another and fingering the hilts of their swords.

"Tell me, do you believe your position to be secure?" Cormac asked the tyrant in a soft voice.

"Who says it isn't?" Bregant demanded suspiciously, glancing at the door.

"Listen," Cormac said. "My dreams have told me the future of all tyrants such as you. Beware the knife at your back, the mole at your feet, and the weapon that breaks in your hands. You will never be safe. Even the hills are crowned with fire, and that fire will come to consume you."

Bregant let out a hollow laugh, and Cormac knew he was afraid. "Kill him," the usurper said.

But as the guards grabbed the blind king, the clattering of hooves in the courtyard below reached them. Bregant gasped, his confidence destroyed. "See who it is!" he shouted.

Cries of alarm and defiance filled the air, and Cormac heard the voices of his former generals raised in challenge.

"Cormac's armies are advancing with torches and they carry Cormac's flag!" a guard warned.

"But they were allied to me!" Bregant exclaimed.

In panic, the treacherous guards and soldiers of the tyrant fled, and Cormac was left to face Bregant alone.

"My prophecy is almost fulfilled," Cormac said.

"You won't murder me. You can't!" Bregant shrieked. "That's not the way King Cormac rules."

"I don't have to," Cormac answered. "You chose your horse, and now it has stumbled."

With a choking cry, Bregant turned to run. But in his terror, he missed his footing, and plunged from the tower to the torch-lit courtyard below.

Cormac heard a rustle of wings and the click of sharp talons on stone. The crow let out one gloating croak and flew away, as the sun rose and crowned Cormac's head with fire.